This book belongs to

....

Five-minute PRINCESS — Tales —

p

CONTENTS

— The — ENCHANTED — Garden —

Princess Sylvie grew up in a beautiful castle, but it had no garden. So she loved to walk through the meadows just to look at the flowers. Princess Sylvie loved flowers!

One day Princess Sylvie found an overgrown path. She asked a woman where the path led.

"That path leads to the garden of the enchantress!" said the woman.

"What is an enchantress?" Princess Sylvie asked.

"Someone who uses magic! So be warned … don't pick the flowers or who knows what terrible things might happen!"

Princess Sylvie followed the path until she came to a small cottage with the prettiest garden she had ever seen! It was filled with flowers of every colour and perfume!

After that, Princess Sylvie went every day. Winter came and snow lay thick, yet the garden stayed the same.

Princess Sylvie forgot all about the enchantress. One wintry day, she picked a rose from the garden and took it back to the castle. As she put it in water, Princess Sylvie suddenly remembered the warning! She'd picked a flower from the enchanted garden and who knew what terrible things might happen?

But days passed and nothing happened. The rose stayed as fresh as the day it was picked. Then months passed and still nothing happened. Forgetting her fears, Princess Sylvie decided to go back to the enchanted garden.

When she saw the garden, Princess Sylvie wanted to cry! The grass was brown. The flowers had withered and died! Then she heard someone weeping. Inside the cottage the enchantress was sitting by the fire, crying. She was old and bent. Although Princess Sylvie was afraid, she felt sorry for her.

"What happened to your lovely garden?" Princess Sylvie asked.

"Someone picked a rose from my magic garden!" said the enchantress. "The rose will live forever, but the rest must die!"

"Can't your magic bring the garden back to life?"

Princess Sylvie asked.

"Alas, when the rose
was picked, my magic
was lost! And now,
I too will wither
and die!"

"What can I do?"
asked Princess Sylvie,
heartbroken.

"Only a princess
can bring my magic back,"
she replied.

"How?" asked Princess Sylvie.

"She must bring me six sacks of stinging nettles!
No princess would do such a thing."

Princess Sylvie didn't say anything. She turned
and ran to the meadow. She gathered up armful after
armful of nettles, not caring that they stung her. She
filled six sacks and took them back to the
enchantress.

"You are kind," she said. "But the nettles must be picked by a princess."

"But I am a princess," said Princess Sylvie.

Without delay, the enchantress made a magic potion with the nettles and drank it. Instantly, the garden became enchanted again! Princess Sylvie gasped! Gone was the bent old lady and in her place was a beautiful young woman.

"My beautiful garden is restored," smiled the enchantress, "and so am I!"

And so the enchantress and the princess became great friends and shared the enchanted garden.

— Princess —
ROSEBUD

In a beautiful palace in a land far away, lived a little princess. The king and queen called her Princess Rosebud, because on her left ankle was a small pink mark in the shape of a rose.

On her third birthday, Princess Rosebud was given a pretty white pony. The princess rode her pony with her nanny and her groom at her side. They went to the edge of the forest then stopped for a rest. The pretty white pony was tied to a tree branch. The nanny and the groom talked

together, while the little princess wandered along a forest path collecting flowers and leaves. They didn't notice how far the little princess had wandered. Soon Princess Rosebud couldn't see her nanny or her groom or her beautiful white pony. She called and called for her nanny. But no one came. It began to get dark. The little princess was scared and began to cry.

Princess Rosebud walked on until she saw a light through the trees. There was a little house with a straw roof and tiny little windows and a small wooden door. Suddenly, the door opened. There stood a little old woman!

Now, the old woman was blind and couldn't see the little princess, but she could hear a small child crying. The old woman was kind. She took the little princess inside and sat her by a warm fire. Then she gave her thin slices of bread and honey, and a glass of milk.

"What is your name, child?" she asked.

"Rosebud," answered the princess.

"Where do you live, child?" she asked.

"I don't know," answered the princess. "I got lost in the forest."

"Well, you can stay with me until someone comes to find you, my dear," said the kind old woman.

Back at the palace, the king and queen were very upset that their only daughter was lost. They offered a reward of a hundred gold coins to anyone who

off! He took her to the palace gate. Rosebud felt she had seen the palace before, but could not remember when. Before dark, the pony returned her to the cottage in the forest.

The next day he came again, and again they visited the palace before returning to the cottage.

Then the next day, the palace gate was open. The pony trotted through the gate just as the king and queen were walking in the gardens. They saw the little girl and the pony and thought she was the prettiest girl they had ever seen.

"What is your name, child?" the queen asked her.

"Rosebud, your majesty," Rosebud replied.

could find her. But many years went by and no one found the little princess. The king and queen thought they would never see the princess again.

Meanwhile Rosebud was very happy living in the forest. She forgot that she had ever been a princess! She forgot she had lived in a palace! She forgot her fine clothes and jewels. She even forgot her white pony!

One day, when she was walking in the garden, a pony galloped into view. He was as white as milk, and had a jewelled saddle and bridle!

Rosebud loved him immediately! She climbed into the saddle, and the pony turned swiftly, and galloped

"Ah," sighed the queen sadly, "that is the name of my long-lost daughter."

Then, just as Rosebud was mounting the pony to ride home, the queen noticed the pink rose on her left ankle!

She stared at it in disbelief!

"Sire!" she cried to the king. "It is our daughter, Princess Rosebud."

The whole kingdom rejoiced to hear that the princess had returned. The king offered the old woman a reward for caring for the princess, but she shook her head.

"I only want to be near Rosebud for the rest of my days," she said. And so the old woman came to live in the palace with Princess Rosebud.

The Princess of

HEARTS

Princess Ruby was given her name because she was born with ruby-red lips the shape of a tiny heart. When she grew up she was very beautiful, with coal-black hair down to her waist, green eyes and skin as pale as milk.

She was a charming and friendly girl, but she insisted that everything she owned was heart-shaped! Her bed was heart-shaped, her table and chair were heart-shaped, her cushions were heart-shaped, even the sandwiches her maid brought her at tea time were cut into the shape of hearts!

As soon as she was old enough, the king and queen wanted Princess Ruby to find a husband.

"There is a prince in the next kingdom who is looking for a wife," they told her. "He is brave and handsome and rich. Everything a princess could wish for."

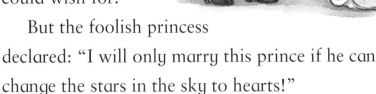

But the foolish princess declared: "I will only marry this prince if he can change the stars in the sky to hearts!"

The king and queen didn't know how to answer!

When Prince Gallant came to visit he was indeed as handsome as her parents had said. Princess Ruby liked his kindly eyes and his pleasant smile.

They spent the afternoon walking in the palace

gardens, and talking about everything under the sun. But Prince Gallant could not promise Princess Ruby that he could change the shape of the stars. So the princess could not marry him!

As she watched the prince ride away, Princess Ruby suddenly wished she had not been so foolish!

Prince Gallant was unhappy, too, as he rode home through the forest. Suddenly, he heard a screeching sound. In the clearing, a dragon was attacking a peacock. Jumping off his horse, the prince took out his sword and chased the dragon away. The peacock was in a sorry state. All his beautiful tail feathers were scattered around him.

"Thank you for saving me," said the peacock. The prince was astonished to hear the peacock talk. "I have magical powers," explained the peacock. "But I am now very weak. The dragon has pulled out some of my magic feathers!"

The prince set to work gathering up all the peacock's feathers. As soon as the feathers had been returned, the peacock gave a loud cry and spread his tail wide. The peacock's tail glowed.

"Before I go, I will grant you a single wish," he told the prince. Prince Gallant wished that the stars in the sky would change into the shape of hearts!

Later that night Princess Ruby was in her bedchamber. She was beginning to regret that she had refused to marry Prince Gallant.

Feeling sad she looked out of the window at the full moon casting its radiant light over the hills and fields beyond the palace.

Then she glanced at the stars – and couldn't believe her eyes!

Every single one was in the shape of a silver heart!

At that moment she saw Prince Gallant riding over the hill. He stopped his horse beneath Princess Ruby's window.

She was overjoyed to see him.

"Will you ever forgive me," she cried, "for being so foolish as to ask you to change the shape of the stars?"

"There is nothing to forgive," said the prince, and again he asked if she would marry him. Filled with delight Princess Ruby, of course, agreed!

They were married on a lovely summer's day. And when Princess Ruby made her wedding vows, she promised never to ask for anything foolish again!

The Pig and
THE JEWELS

Daisy was as pretty as a picture. She was very kind too. Daisy looked after all the animals on the farm where she lived. She loved them all dearly, and the animals all loved her too.

But Daisy dreamt of being more than a farmer's daughter. As she fed the hens and the ducks or counted the sheep, Daisy day-dreamed about being a princess. At night when she lay in bed she would say to herself, "Oh, how I wish I could be a princess!"

One day she found a sick pig

at the edge of the forest. She carried him to the farm and nursed him until he was better. The pig became her favourite animal, and he followed her wherever she went.

She told him all her secrets, and he listened carefully, his little eyes fixed on hers. It was almost as if he understood everything she said. She even told him the most important secret of all.

"Dear little pig," she whispered in his ear, " I wish, I wish I could be a princess!"

That night the pig went away. When he returned the next morning, he had a tiara made of precious jewels on his head. The pig stood in front of Daisy, the jewels glinting in the sunshine.

"Darling pig," cried Daisy, "is that for me?"

The pig grunted. Daisy took the tiara and put it on her head. It fitted her perfectly.

The next night the pig went away again. In the morning he returned as before, this time with a beautiful necklace. Daisy put it on.

"How do I look?" she asked him. But of course the pig just grunted.

After that the pig went away every night for six nights. And every morning for six mornings he returned with something different.

First he brought a dress of white silk, followed by

a crimson cloak and soft leather shoes. Then bracelets set with jewels, and long lengths of satin ribbon for her hair. And, finally, a ring made of gold and rubies.

Daisy put on all the gifts the pig had brought her and stood in front of a long mirror.

"At last," she whispered to her reflection, "I look just like a real princess."

The next day the pig disappeared again. Daisy didn't worry because she knew he always returned. But days went by and then weeks, and the pig did not return. Daisy missed him more than she could say.

The days grew short and snow lay in deep drifts on the ground. Daisy spent the evenings sitting by the fire in her white silk dress and crimson cloak. Her heart was sad and heavy when she thought about her dear, lost pig.

"I would be happy just to remain a farmer's daughter if only he would return to me," she cried, watching the logs burn in the hearth.

Suddenly there was a noise at the door – it was the pig! With a cry of joy she bent to kiss him and, as she did, he turned into a handsome prince! Daisy gasped with amazement.

"Sweet Daisy," said the prince taking her hand. "If it wasn't for you I would still be alone and friendless, wandering in the forest."

He explained how a wicked witch had cast a spell on him to turn him into a pig. "Your kiss broke the spell," said the prince. "Daisy, will you marry me?"

It was a dream come true. At long last, Daisy really was going to become Princess Daisy!

— The —
PRINCESS
Who Never Smiled

A long time ago, in a far-off land, a princess was born. The king and queen called her Princess Columbine. They thought she was the most precious child ever to be born. And, to make sure that she was watched over every minute of every day, they hired a nurse to look after her.

One day, the queen came to the nursery and found the nurse asleep and the little princess crying. The queen was very cross and called for the king. He told off the nurse for not watching the baby.

But what the king and queen didn't know was that the nurse was really a wicked enchantress. The angry enchantress cast a spell over the little baby princess:

"Princess Columbine will never smile again until she learns my real name!"

The king and queen were devastated. From that day on, the princess never smiled! Names were collected from all over the land. They tried all the usual names such as Jane, Catherine, Amanda. They tried more unusual names such as Araminta, Tallulah, Leanora. They even tried quite outlandish names such as Dorominty, Truditta, Charlottamina. But none broke the spell.

Princess Columbine grew up to be a sweet and beautiful girl. Everybody loved her. But her face was always so sad, it made the king and queen unhappy. They tried everything to make her smile. They bought her a puppy. They even hired a court jester who told the silliest jokes you've ever heard.

"Why did the pecans cross the road?" asked the jolly jester. The princess shrugged.

"Because they were nuts!" the jester laughed.

"Why did the ice-cream?" the jester tried again. The princess just gazed politely.

"Because the jelly wobbled!"

One day an artist called Rudolpho came to the palace and asked the king if he could paint the princess's portrait. The king agreed on one condition.

He had to paint the
princess smiling.
Rudolpho set up his
easel beneath a
large mirror and
began straight
away. The
princess sat
opposite
watching him
paint in the mirror
behind him. As he
worked, Rudolpho
asked the princess about
all the people in the palace. He had soon painted the
princess's portrait, all except for her smile. But he
couldn't make the princess smile.

Rudolpho tried some funny drawings. He drew
silly pictures of the king and queen. The princess
looked on politely. Then he drew a picture of her old

nurse and gave her a moustache, and over it he wrote NURSE. Princess Columbine gazed in the mirror. There, over the picture, was the word NURSE spelled out back to front – ƎƧЯUИ.

"ESRUN," Princess Columbine said quietly. And then she smiled. "Her name is ESRUN!" laughed Princess Columbine. At last the spell was broken! The king and queen heard her laughter and came rushing to see what was happening. They were so happy that soon everyone in the palace was laughing too.

The Tale of Two
PRINCESSES

Long ago there were twin princesses called Charmina and Charlotte. Even though they were twins, the princesses were very different. In fact they were opposites. Princess Charmina was gracious and charming to everyone. She curtsied politely to the king and queen. And she stood quite still while the royal dressmakers came to fit her new ball gown.

Princess Charlotte was very different!

"Why do I have to dress like a puffball?" grumbled Princess Charlotte when it was her turn to have a new ball gown fitted.

"How dare you speak to us like that!" her parents cried.

But she did dare. She dared to run barefoot through the gardens until her hair looked like a bush. She dared to wear her shabbiest clothes. In fact, she didn't behave like a princess at all!

One day there was to be a ball at the palace. The guests of honour were two princes from the next kingdom. The two princesses, dressed in their new ball gowns, kept getting in the way of the preparations. "Why don't you go for a walk until our guests arrive?" suggested the queen. "But stay together, don't get dirty and don't be late!"

The two princesses walked to the bottom of the palace gardens.

"Let's go into the forest," said Princess Charlotte to her sister.

"I don't think we should," said Princess Charmina. "Our gowns will get dirty." But Princess Charlotte had already set off.

"Wait for me!" called Princess Charmina. "We must stay together!" They wandered deeper and deeper into the forest. They crunched through fallen leaves, listening to the birds singing.

"I think we should go back," Princess Charmina told her sister. "We'll be late for the ball."

Just then they heard a strange noise.

"Let's turn back!" said Princess Charmina, afraid.

"It may be someone in distress!" said Princess Charlotte. "We must go and help!"

Although Princess Charmina was scared, she agreed. "But we must get back in time for the ball."

"Don't worry, we will," said Princess Charlotte.

They set off again going even deeper into the forest. Finally, they came upon two horses in a clearing, but there was no sign of their riders. Just then they heard voices calling out,

"Who's there?"

At first, the two princesses couldn't see where the voices were coming from. In the middle of the clearing there was a large pit – an old bear trap. They peered over the edge. Princess Charmina clapped her hand over her mouth in astonishment. Princess Charlotte burst out laughing. There at the bottom of the pit were two princes.

"How do you do?" said the first prince.

"Well, don't just stand there," said the second prince. "Help us out!"

The two princesses found ropes and threw one end down to the princes. They tied the other end to their horses. Soon the princes were rescued and laughed with the princesses. They all set off to the palace together.

On their return they found everyone in the palace in a state of panic. The king and queen were angry when their daughters returned late looking so dirty. But their anger turned to joy when the two princes explained what had happened.

Everyone enjoyed the ball. The two princesses danced all night with the two princes. And, do you know, from that time on, Charlotte paid more attention to her gowns and hair. And Charmina became a little more playful and daring than before!

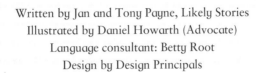

Written by Jan and Tony Payne, Likely Stories
Illustrated by Daniel Howarth (Advocate)
Language consultant: Betty Root
Design by Design Principals

This is a Parragon Book
First published 2002

Parragon
Queen Street House
4 Queen Street
Bath BA1 1HE, UK

Printed in Spain

ISBN 0-75258-593-2